Schoolies™

The Talent Show

Based on the characters created by
Ellen Crimi-Trent

priddy books

One morning, Mrs Hedge asked the Schoolies an interesting question.

Then Chip spoke up.

Mrs Hedge told the Schoolies that soon there would be a School Talent Show. Everyone was looking forward to it, especially Chip!

Each of the Schoolies practised their talents for the show. Hayden Hoot added numbers.

Spencer tried tricks on his roller skates.

Chip practised singing.
He sang, and sang, and sang.

Leeza loved to perform, but her sister Lydia was shy and didn't want to be in the Talent Show. So Mrs Hedge gave Lydia a special job.

Soon it was time for the Talent Show. The Schoolies' families came to watch.

The Schoolies were very excited.

First, it was Hayden's turn
to show his talent.

Then, Leeza performed the part of a princess.

Spencer did a roller skating trick.

Then C.J. Crawley painted a picture, while Kitty played piano. Backstage, Chip started to feel nervous.

Soon, it was time for Chip to sing.
He went out onto the stage.

Mrs Hedge started to play
the music, but when Chip tried
to sing, no words came out.

Poor Chip was feeling so nervous,
he couldn't sing at all!

Lydia saw that Chip was afraid, so she whispered to her friend.

Chip nodded.
Lydia took a deep breath,
then she walked on stage
and held Chip's hand.

Together, they began to sing.

Soon all the Schoolies were singing together. Everybody in the audience clapped.

At the end of the show, Chip and Lydia took a bow together.